ELSIE
TIMES EIGHT

ELSIE
TIMES EIGHT

Story and Pictures by

NATALIE BABBITT

Michael di Capua Books

Hyperion Books for Children

This book is for
Margaret Billings Frattaroli,
my second grandchild

Elsie's fairy godmother loved her very much and came by once in a while to see how things were going.

One day Elsie's mama said, "Elsie has been such a good girl lately! You know, she didn't always do the things she should, before."

Elsie's fairy godmother meant well, but sometimes she heard things wrong. "Elsie should be four?" she thought to herself. "Dear me! Still, I guess I could do it."

So she waved her wand and changed the one Elsie into four Elsies.

This was a great surprise to Elsie and her mama and papa. It also surprised the cat.

As Elsie's fairy godmother was leaving, Papa ran after her and called, "No! WAIT!"

"Eight! That *is* a number," thought Elsie's fairy godmother. "Still, I guess I could do it."

So she waved her wand again and changed the four Elsies
into eight Elsies.

And then she was gone.

What a time it was after that! For there was only one cat. In fact, there was only one of everything. The Elsies fought over all of it, and the noise was astonishing.

Papa had to bring in eight times as many vegetables from the garden, and Mama had to cook eight times as much for dinner. And there was only one chair for one Elsie.

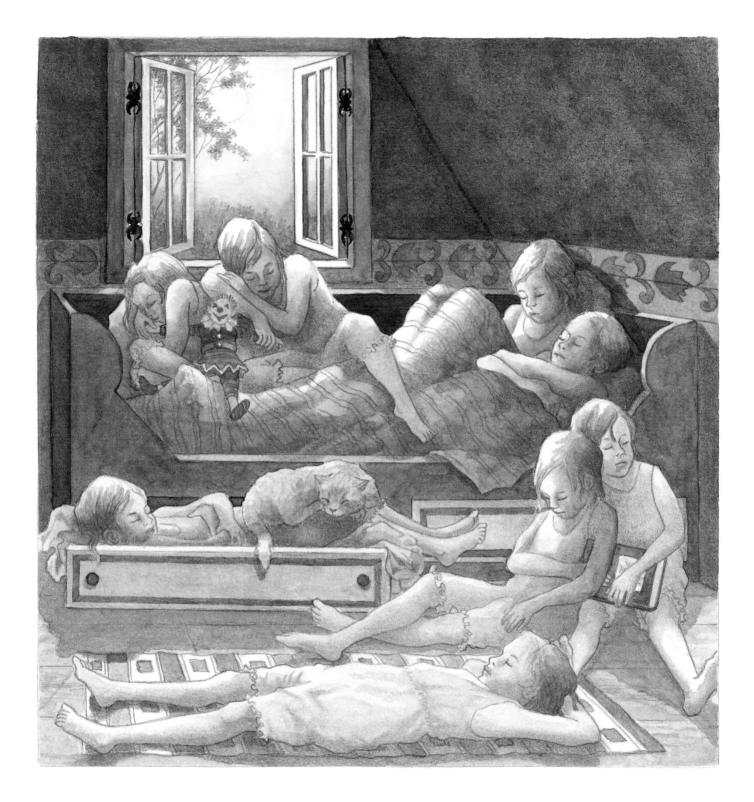

When it was time for bed, Papa and Mama couldn't keep
track of which Elsies they had hugged and which they hadn't.
And of course there was only one bed for one Elsie.

Day after day, the Elsies were noisy. It made the goats nervous, and annoyed the neighbors.

All the birds went somewhere else, and the cat was not pleased with it, either.

At last the Mayor came to the door. "You will have to do something about this rowdydow and racket," he said to Mama. "People are complaining."

But the Elsies paid no attention. They chased him away, and then they fought over his hat.

The Mayor sent a brave man with a message. It said, "Please return my hat. And you must move to another place at once, a place very far from here."

"It's that silly fairy godmother's fault," said Papa.

"There, there," said Mama. "She meant well. She'll set it all straight in a minute when we tell her."

But they didn't know where she was, so they had to do as they were told. When everything was packed, they gathered the goats, the cat, and the Elsies, and started off.

They walked and walked till they came to a new town far down the road, but nobody wanted them to stay there, for the Elsies were too noisy. So they had to keep on going.

At last they saw Elsie's fairy godmother sitting in a tree.
"What's this?" she asked them. "Why are you moving?"
"Eight Elsies were too many for the old place," said Mama.

en I'll just change them back to one," said Elsie's fairy

ther. "But which one? Which is the first Elsie?"

ld think *you* would know," said Papa.

ind," said Mama.

Just then, however, a dog came by and barked at the
The cat was so alarmed that it ran to one of the Els
jumped into her arms.

"Aha!" said Papa. "The *cat* knows who's who." So Elsie's fairy godmother changed the eight Elsies back into the one holding the cat. For this was indeed the first Elsie. Cats never make mistakes.

"Next time," said Papa to Elsie's fairy godmother, "do try to hear things right. Goats you need more of, but one Elsie is enough. Even one cat ought to be plenty."

But Elsie's fairy godmother heard it wrong. *"Twenty?"* she said to herself. "Oh well, I guess I could do it." So before she flew away, she changed the one cat into twenty.

This was a great surprise to everyone, but not a bad surprise. Elsie liked it, and the cat was glad for the company.

And when they came home again, the neighbors were delighted. After all, twenty cats can manage quite a lot of mice.

So all the trouble was over.
Elsie's fairy godmother tried not to hear things
wrong again, and everyone lived quietly ever after.

But Elsie always knew which was the first cat.

(As for the mice, they had to pack up and move,
for mice do not like to be managed.)